Dora's Picnic

by Christine Ricci
illustrated by Susan Hall

Ready-to-Read

Simon Spotlight/Nick Jr.

New York   London   Toronto   Sydney   Singapore

Based on the TV series *Dora the Explorer*® as seen on Nick Jr.®

SIMON SPOTLIGHT
An imprint of Simon & Schuster Children's Publishing Division
1230 Avenue of the Americas,
New York, New York 10020

4 6 8 10 9 7 5 3

Ricci, Christine.
Dora's picnic / by Christine Ricci.
p. cm.—(Ready-to-read. Level 1, Dora the explorer ; 1)
Summary: Dora and her animal friends all contribute something to bring to
a picnic at Play Park. Features rebuses.
ISBN 0-689-85238-X
1. Rebuses. [1. Picnicking—Fiction. 2. Animals—Fiction. 3. Parks—Fiction. 4. Rebuses.]
I. Title. II. Series.
PZ7.R355 Do 2003
[E]—dc21
2002004518

Hi! I am . We are
going to a picnic at Play
Park! Play Park has a 🪜,
SLIDE
a 📦, and 🛝.
SANDBOX   SWINGS

My **mami** is helping me make  PEANUT-BUTTER -and- JELLY sandwiches for the picnic.

 BOOTS is my best friend.

He loves !
BANANAS

 BOOTS has a bunch of 🍌 **BANANAS**
for the picnic.

BENNY is riding his **BICYCLE** to the picnic.

He is carrying juice

APPLE

in his .

BASKET

Here comes the .
BIG RED CHICKEN

The has a big of
BIG RED CHICKEN   BAG

 for the picnic.
POPCORN

Yummy!

Look!  has a bowl of

BABY BLUE BIRD

fruit in her  .

WAGON

The fruit bowl has ,
BANANAS

, and .
APPLES   GRAPES

What did  bring to the picnic?

TICO

 brought .
TICO   BREAD

The **is filled with**
BREAD

and **!**
BLUEBERRIES   NUTS

ISA made **CUPCAKES** to share with everyone.

I like chocolate
CUPCAKES

with ___ icing. What kind
PINK

do you like?

Look out for 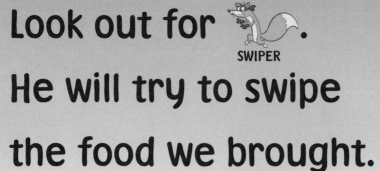.

He will try to swipe

the food we brought.

 is hiding behind
the .

SWIPER

TREE

Say, "Swiper, no swiping!"
Yay! You stopped !

SWIPER

We made it to Play Park! This  is perfect for

TABLE

our picnic. But first we

want to play!

likes to go down

the .

is making a

BABY BLUE BIRD   SAND CASTLE

in the **.**

SANDBOX

The pushes

BIG RED CHICKEN   BOOTS

and  on the .

ISA   SWINGS

This is the best picnic!
We can all share the food.
What would **you** bring
to a picnic?